6

TIZZ TAKES A TRIP

By ELISA BIALK

Illustrated by Dwight Mutchler

CHILDRENS PRESS, Chicago

For

Elena and Elisabeth,

who taught me all about girls like Tracy

THIS EDITION PRINTED 1963

T IS FOR TIZZ

In the middle of a pleasant dream, Tracy Hill heard the alarm go off in her parents' room, which was next to her own. She lay in her warm bed for a long moment, enjoying waking up slowly.

Then, suddenly, she thought of Tizz. In an instant, Tracy was wide awake. Leaping out of bed, she ran to the window and looked outside.

There, in the new corral built near the house, Tizz was prancing about, her white mane streaming in the early November wind. It was a cold wind, Tracy could tell as she leaned out of the window, but she was in cozy pajamas and did not mind.

"Tizz," she called, "how do you get up so early? Do you have an alarm clock, too?"

Tizz turned her head in the direction of

Tracy's voice, for all the world as if she were thinking over what her young owner had said. Then the pretty cream-colored pony shook her mane, kicked up her heels, and raced friskily over to the shed, where her feed bin stood empty.

Tracy laughed out loud. "All right," she called, "I can take a hint! I'll be down in a minute."

She closed the window and quickly got into the wool skirt and sweater her mother had helped her lay out the night before. Hurrying, she beat her older brother, Don, into the bathroom, so that she could wash up and brush her teeth. The only help she needed then was a combing from her mother, to get out the snarls that *would* get into her blond pony tail during the night.

Don, who was wearing his Cub Scout uniform because there would be a Den meeting, came out to the corral. Tizz was loudly munching away at her breakfast. "You sure were up early this morning!" he complained. "How early do I have to get up, if I want to feed Tizz myself!"

"Pretty early," Tracy told him as she patted the pony's neck with a hand that was warm with love. "Tizz gets hungry early. She told me when I looked out the window."

"She *told* you!" Don scoffed. "Ponies can't talk!"

"Tizz can," Tracy insisted. It was something of a family joke that Tracy truly believed Tizz did talk. As a matter of fact, Tracy loved the pony so much and spent so much time with her, that she had come to know the meaning of every neigh and whinny, and every swish of Tizz's tail. It *seemed* as if the pony could talk.

Don was looking around the corral while he and his sister were talking. "This sure is a nice corral," he commented. "I'm glad we finally got it. Remember all the trouble we had, trying to keep Tizz home, before?"

Tracy nodded. "She was awfully smart about breaking loose, wasn't she?"

"Smart, yes, but look all the trouble she caused. We were always out looking for her, and so were our friends and neighbors."

"Shh, Don, you'll hurt her feelings!" Tracy said in a soft voice, looking into Tizz's big brown eyes.

"Aw, she's only a pony."

"Only a pony!" Tracy echoed in such a hurt voice that Don quickly added, "Of course, she's a pretty wonderful pony!"

"She's the smartest pony in the world," Tracy insisted, hugging her. "And the prettiest, too." She had said that all along, from the moment her grandmother had brought Tizz home as a big surprise.

"Sure, she is," Don agreed. "All the same, I'm glad we've got the corral." Then he cried out: "Hey, do you know what?"

"What?"

"We never did have that party we were going to have, for all the kids and parents who helped build the corral!"

"That's right, we didn't." Tracy spoke slowly. She had been so happy with Tizz and the nice corral that she had forgotten all about it.

"We'll have to talk to Mom and Dad about

it," Don pointed out. "Not now, though. I've got to meet Greg and Johnny before school."

"I've got to be there early, too," Tracy said. "Sue and Helen and I are working on a project together." It made her feel very important to be able to say that. When she had first started going to the new school in September, Tracy had found it a little hard to make friends right away. But now she knew everyone in her class, and Tizz had helped her get acquainted.

She gave Tizz a last loving pat, promised to come right home after school, and ran into the house for a second to say goodby to her mother.

Then she hurried after Don, who was taking the short cut across the fields.

When the Hills had first moved to the new house, the fields all around were green and high with grass. Now they were brown and stubbly, with little crackly ponds of thin ice scattered here and there. It was fun to step upon the ice, and see the cobwebs of little lines spin out rapidly all around their footprints.

Miss Brown, Tracy's teacher, was wearing a

bright blue sweater and skirt this morning. Tracy liked it very much, and said so. When she had first come to school she had been rather shy, but now she always spoke up nicely.

Soon after the bell, the boys and girls gathered together in a big circle, waiting for Miss Brown to start the reading period. The teacher took up the book she was holding in her lap. "Now, children," she said in her gentle, pleasant voice, "we're going to start a new book this morning. But first I would like to ask you—what do you think T stands for?"

"Tizz," Tracy answered promptly. Some of the other children nodded and agreed, "Yes, Tizz."

Miss Brown smiled. "T does stand for Tizz, that's true, but it happens that I was not thinking of Tizz at the moment." With a special smile for Tracy, she added, "I hope Tracy will forgive me, but there's something else that's important, too. What else does T stand for"?

Paul suggested, "Thanksgiving?"

Miss Brown nodded. "Yes, that's right. Thanksgiving is coming soon, and I thought we might read this story about the Pilgrims. Then, we are going to have a wonderful treat. In a few days, we are all going over to the Pioneer Room at the Central School."

"Hurray!" the children cried, clapping their hands. Most of them knew about the Pioneer Room through their older brothers and sisters. Even Tracy, the newest girl in the class, had heard about it.

"First, I think we should learn more about the Pilgrims, and the pioneers who settled our country," Miss Brown was saying.

Tracy nodded, as the other boys and girls were nodding, but to tell the truth, her mind was wandering a little.

She was thinking.

T is for Tizz
   and Tizz is for Tracy.

It gave her a warm feeling, just to think about how close she and Tizz were to each other.

HOW ABOUT THAT PARTY?

Tracy had another warm feeling later in the day when she sat in the kitchen while her mother was cooking dinner. Next to her rides with Tizz, she thought this was the nicest time of the day. Not only because the kitchen smelled so good, but because she and her mother could talk together while they waited for Don to get home from a Cub Scout meeting, or listened for Mr. Hill's car to come up the road.

Yet even though Tracy enjoyed this quiet half hour with her mother very much, she still thought, and often talked, about Tizz. Now she was asking, "You don't think it will be too cold for Tizz out in the corral during the winter, do you, Mother?"

Mrs. Hill, who was a pretty, taller edition of Tracy, smiled as she turned some lamb chops she was broiling. "Goodness, no! She's got a shed out there for shelter, too, you know."

"Yes, but the shed isn't heated."

Mrs. Hill's smile rippled into a laugh. "Ponies don't need steam-heated quarters. Why, out West they live out-of-doors all winter long, in below-zero weather. They manage to forage for their own food, too."

"Tizz has a warm thick coat," Tracy reminded herself. "I'll bet it's this thick." She spread her fingers wide apart.

"Well—perhaps not quite *that* thick, but it is good and warm, all right," her mother agreed. She turned away from the range, asking, "Do I hear a familiar sound?"

"Daddy!" Tracy cried. She flew to the door to greet him as he came in, a tall man with curly dark hair and a young-looking face that had crinkles around the eyes from smiling so much.

"Hi, Tracy!" he greeted her, swinging her up as if she weighed nothing, and giving her a hug and a kiss. "What did Tizz have to tell you today?"

"Oh, lots of things," Tracy answered as seriously as if her father were not teasing. "We talked mostly about how cold she might get in the wintertime."

"Now, I hope you're not going to worry about *that!*" he grinned. "I'll put my foot down on one thing—she's not going to sleep in your bed no matter how cold it gets!"

Tracy laughed with him, knowing he was joking.

He set her down to greet her mother, and before he could ask, "Where's Don?" there was a scurrying of footsteps up the walk, and Don came in panting.

"Sorry to be late," Don apologized. "Our Den meeting ran a little late today. We were all working on a new project and—." The sentence dangled as he searched for words to explain.

"Yes, I know." Mr. Hill nodded. "I remember some of those projects myself, and I know how time can get away from you. But better wash up, fellow. Looks to me as if dinner's just about ready."

Mrs. Hill took the nicely browned chops out of the oven, and put them on the plates with baked potatoes and bright green peas. "Yes, we're all set. But those hands have got to be clean!" she warned.

"They'll be clean," Don promised. His voice sounded as if it was coming from a distance. It was, as a matter of fact, because he was already upstairs, on his way to the bathroom. Boys move pretty fast.

It was a well-scrubbed and shiny Don who brought up an important matter at the dinner table. "You know what?" He came to the point quickly. "We never did have that party for the kids and parents who helped us build the corral!"

There was a moment of silence while his parents exchanged a glance. Then Mr. Hill said quietly: " 'Never did' means a long time. The corral has only been up a few weeks."

"Even so," Don insisted. "We ought to have that party."

"Your father and I have talked about it several times," Mrs. Hill spoke up from her end of the table.

"Well, then let's have it!" Don's eager voice urged.

Tracy clapped her hands. "I could make a corsage of carrots for Tizz. She'd be the belle of the ball!"

"Yes," Mr. Hill agreed, "she'd be the belle of the ball, all right—but we may have to wait awhile to hold that ball."

"Aw, Dad," Don protested. "Why can't we have that party now?"

Mr. Hill dipped into his buttery baked potato before he spoke. "For a very simple reason, Don. We can't afford it. Parties cost money. We'd have to have a pretty big one, to invite all of those people who helped us build the corral. Right now, we're counting our pennies."

"Moving into a new home means many extra expenses," Mrs. Hill explained. She looked from Don to Tracy and back to Don again. "I'm sure you children understand."

"Sure, we understand," Don said slowly. "But will the kids and their parents understand? We told them we were going to have a party."

"We'll have it all right," Mr. Hill promised. "Only, we'll have to wait awhile. Maybe 'til after the holidays."

"Oh, we don't want to wait that long!" Don cried. "It's not even Thanksgiving yet." His face lighted up suddenly. "Say, I've got an idea! Why can't we earn the money for that party?"

"That's all right with me," Tracy agreed, "but how could we earn it?"

The idea struck Don so hard that he jumped up from the table. "I know! I'll get a paper route! Why, Greg makes over four dollars a week on his."

"Now, wait a minute," Mr. Hill advised. "Simmer down. That sounds like a good idea, but having a paper route means a lot of work. You've got to get up awfully early in the morning, and to earn that much money, you'd have to have a pretty big route."

"If Greg can do it, so can I," Don insisted.

"You're smarter than Greg," Tracy added loyally.

"I don't know if I'm smarter," said Don, "but I can run as fast."

"You can't run miles every morning on a paper route," his father pointed out sensibly.

"I can ride my bicycle."

"Not when the snow comes to stay."

"I can—"

Out in the corral, Tizz, seeing the lights in the house, gave a lonesome whinny.

Tracy's wide blue eyes met Don's bright brown ones across the table. A message was delivered between them, and it was a message not from Tracy, but from Tizz. This time, Don was the one who was willing to claim that Tizz actually could talk!

"I can ride Tizz!" he shouted. "She just said so."

"Well," Mr. Hill murmured, looking surprised, "we'll see."

But Tracy and Don already were talking

about it as excitedly as if it were all settled. To them, it seemed like a wonderful idea.

INVITATION TO GRANDMA'S

After school the very next day, Don went over to the news agency. He talked to the manager about getting a newspaper route.

"You're pretty young, aren't you?" the manager, Mr. Nelson, asked.

"I'm going on ten," Don answered. That sounded much older than to say he was nine.

The manager said thoughtfully, "H'mmm . . . We have a couple of boys as young as you are, and one of our best girls isn't ten yet, either."

"Girls? Do you have girls delivering papers?"

"Yes, we have about seven or eight. They do a good job, too."

"Then I guess it's all right if my sister helps me?"

"Yes, that's perfectly all right. But first we'll

have to wait until there's a route open. Right now they're all taken. What's your name?"

"Don Hill."

"Where do you live?"

When Don told him, Mr. Nelson looked up from the card he was filling out. "I'm sorry, but I don't think you could get a paper route close to your house. You live in what we consider a rural district, and we have a man who delivers papers there by jeep."

"You mean the houses are too scattered to get around by bicycle?"

The manager nodded. "In the winter, you can't use a bike, and it's too much distance to cover by foot."

Don's smile spread across his bright-looking face. "That doesn't worry me a bit, Mr. Nelson. I could deliver the papers by pony."

"By pony? Do you have one?"

"Sure. Her name is Tizz. She belongs to me and Tracy—that's my sister. My grandmother gave her to us."

The manager was smiling broadly. "I see.

The Pony Express, eh?"

"Can I get the job, mister?" Don asked eagerly.

"I'll have to talk to the man who's got the route now, and see if we can do some switching around."

"Look, Mr. Nelson," Don said coaxingly, "couldn't we have the job for just a couple of weeks? My sister and I want to earn some money."

"I'll see what I can do. Drop in again later in the week."

Don sped home. Tracy was out riding Tizz, but he could see her across the fields, so he ran to meet her.

"Tracy," he shouted, "I'm going to get that paper route, and you can help me."

Tracy's face shone with pleasure. She loved to share experiences with Don. "When do we start?"

"We'll have to wait until a route is open. But it won't be long, I'll bet," he added as her face fell.

Tracy's hand found its way to Tizz's mane

lovingly. "Tizz, will you mind getting up early?"

"She's always up early," Don laughed. "I'm the one who'll mind! What about you? Will you be able to get up real early every morning?"

Tracy thought of that pleasant time she liked to have, waking up slowly in her warm and cozy bed. "I won't mind," she decided bravely.

Don gave Tizz's withers an affectionate slap. "Tizz, you'll be the only paper-delivering pony in town!"

Tizz shook her head smartly, and gave a little whinny. It was as if the children had passed on their excitement to her.

"Let's go in and tell Mother!" Don cried.

He leaped on Tizz's back, behind Tracy, and Tizz trotted home, happily unconcerned with her double burden.

Mrs. Hill was baking apples for dessert, and the kitchen was full of the yummy fragrance of fruit and sugar and cinnamon. Tracy allowed Don to tell about his talk with the news agency manager without cutting in. Then she asked,

"Isn't that wonderful, Mother?"

"Yes," Mrs. Hill agreed. "I think it will be a very good experience for both of you. I know something else that's wonderful, too."

"What is it?" both children asked at once.

"Let's wait until dinnertime, when Daddy will be with us," Mrs. Hill suggested.

As soon as Mr. Hill came home and dinner was on the table, Tracy begged, "Now, can you tell us, Mother?"

"Yes, I'll be happy to. We have a letter from Grandma. She wants us to come down to the farm for Thanksgiving."

"Hurray!" Don shouted.

Tracy said more quietly, "But what about Tizz, mother? We can't leave her home alone."

Her father chuckled. "I could have bet you'd say that."

Her mother seconded his words with a nod. "Yes, Grandma thought of that, too. Here, let me read what she said in her letter."

Mrs. Hill picked up the letter which she had placed in front of her on the table, and read:

"I'm sure Tracy wouldn't leave Tizz, so why not bring the pony along? You can rent a trailer quite cheaply, and I shall insist on paying the rental, as my Thanksgiving present to the children."

This time it was Tracy who shouted loudly, "Hurray!"

"Sounds like a lot of trouble, carting a pony around," Mr. Hill grumbled, but the grumble soon disappeared as he went on to say, "Yet maybe we could—it's not too far—only a half day's trip."

They talked about the trip all through dinner, making plans. Tracy, who loved her grandparents and the farm, too, wondered how she could possibly wait several weeks until it was time to go.

As soon as she had helped her mother clear the table and wash the dishes, Tracy hurried out to the corral. She spoke out loud as she said goodnight to her beloved pony.

"Tizz, you're coming along with us to Grandma's

for Thanksgiving! We're going to have a wonderful time."

Tizz nodded her head. She was as certain of it as Tracy was. When you are a small pretty girl or a small pretty pony, all times are wonderful.

THE PIONEER ROOM

Miss Brown greeted the children with a mysterious smile a few mornings later.

"This is the day," she said when they were all together. "We are going to the Pioneer Room."

The news was greeted with much joy. All the boys and girls knew that a real treat was in store for them.

The school bus came in a little while, to take them to the Central School of the suburb. Going on a bus trip was exciting in itself. The bus driver's name was Tony, and he was a friendly man who told funny stories.

Central School was quite large. Tracy thought it beautiful, but she liked her smaller school better. Yet she knew that Central School had some very special things about it, like the

Pioneer Room they were about to visit.

The room was a big one, off in a corner by itself. It looked like the inside of a log cabin. There was a fireplace with a pot hanging from it, and a long wooden table with benches. There was also a big old-fashioned four-poster bed with a small bed that slipped under it called a "trundle." Dishes and pots and pans were copies of the kind used by pioneers.

All the children had come into the Pioneer Room and were looking around. Miss Brown said, "Now, girls, you can go over there to those hooks and pick out a dress to wear. And you boys go over to that big chest and find your pioneer clothes."

The boys and girls scattered quickly. Tracy selected a blue gingham dress trimmed in white rickrack. When she changed into it, she felt like a different person in the long full skirt and the big puffed sleeves. As a matter of fact, when she looked around at the rest of the children, they all looked different, too. The girls in their pioneer dresses seemed quite grownup. The

boys, wearing deerskin jackets and coonskin hats, looked strange at first. But no one looked strange for long, because the clothes fitted so well into this room where the children were pretending they were living.

First, it was decided who would be the mother and the father, and who would be the children of the make-believe family. Tracy was voted to be the little girl. Sue was the mother and Paul, the tallest boy in the room, was the father. Then it was decided who would be neighbors, who would be the hunters, who would be the preacher—who would play the different parts of the people living in the early settlement.

Because there had been few schools in the pioneer days, the "children" of the family did not go off to a schoolhouse for their instruction. Instead, they stayed at home and sat around the fireplace where the best light was, learning sums and the alphabet. As she studied at the fireplace, Tracy thought this was fun for make-believe, but she knew that she would rather go to her present-day schoolroom where she could learn so much more, and faster. Also, she could be with her friends. Being a pioneer child must have been rather lonely, she thought.

While she was working with her sums, the other boys and girls were busy pretending, too. The "mother" and the "older girls" started to prepare lunch. It would take a long time, because they were going to bake cornbread in the open fire, and cook bacon in a long-handled frying pan held over the flames.

The boys who were pretending to be hunters went out-of-doors, carrying make-believe shooting irons. They went about their business very seriously even though they were just pretending. It was easy to take it seriously when they realized that the pioneers had to depend upon hunting for food, and that when game was scarce, people went hungry.

The morning came to a close all too quickly, but the children were ready for the hot meal which they ate at the long narrow slab table. The cornbread and bacon tasted awfully good, although Tracy found it rather different from the way it tasted at home. Still, she felt that cornbread with dark spots on the bottom, from where it had stuck to the iron pan, and bacon hanging limply from a two-pronged fork, could be very good for a change.

Those who had not worked before had a turn at the chores when it came to dishwashing. Tracy, who often told her mother she wished they had a dishwasher, realized that washing dishes the modern way was not so bad after all. Here, she had to carry the water first from a make-believe well, then heat it at the fireplace, then wash the dishes at the table which had to be cleared first of the luncheon remains. It took quite a long time.

When the dishes were cleared up, the furniture was changed around to make the Pioneer Room seem like a meeting-house. The benches were lined up in a row, so that everyone could sit down. The boy who was playing the preacher conducted a simple Sunday service. Tracy really felt as if she were in church, and even found herself wondering whether any Indians might be lurking around when it would be time to go back home.

After the church service, all of the "neighbors" stopped to visit, making the most of this social time which often had been the only social time for the hardworking pioneers. Tracy liked the way the families stayed together, and the way the neighbors offered to help each other. She overheard two neighbors talk about getting together for a barn-raising, and it was with a sorry feeling that she realized they would not really do it, that this was only a part of the make-believe.

The day ended with an event that would have been very special in the life of the pioneers. The harvest was in, crops had been good, for the moment the Indians were peaceful, and it looked as if the people of the settlement were going to be able to enjoy a winter of plenty. A square dance would be held by way of celebration.

The meeting-hall was used for the party.

This time the benches were pushed back against the walls, making a quadrangle. Miss Brown, who was wearing a pioneer costume, too, so that she fitted perfectly into the background, pretended to be the preacher's wife who could play the organ.

All of the families of the community came in together, the mothers and fathers with the children. Jimmy became the square-dance caller, and did a very good job, too. The children knew only one set, which they had learned in Rhythms, but one set was enough.

The square-dance was still going on, with everyone having a wonderful time, when suddenly a bell sounded, seeming to be very far away. At first no one paid any attention to it, but presently Miss Brown stopped playing the little organ, and said:

"Children, I'm sorry, but that was the bell. School is over."

School? Tracy blinked in surprise at the word. She had completely forgotten that she was actually going to school. To her, as to the

other boys and girls, it had seemed as if she were really living back in the pioneer days.

No one said very much as they got out of the pioneer clothing, but they all looked very sad.

"Don't feel so badly about it," Miss Brown comforted them as they walked to the waiting bus. "We'll come back to the Pioneer Room again some time."

"I wanted to stay there now," Sue said, and some of the other youngsters echoed her wish.

But not Tracy. In her own clothes again, she was back in her own world. She had loved every minute of the day—but had she lived back in pioneer times, she could not have had Tizz!

When she got off the bus, she ran home eagerly, to tell her experience to her mother and Don, and later to her father. But especially to Tizz. Tizz, she knew, would understand exactly how she had felt during the day, not in a room of Central School, but in a pioneer cabin, and a meeting-house, and at an old-time square dance. Tizz would nod her head as if to say,

"Yes, I know it was great fun—but now, how about a carrot?"

THE PAPER ROUTE

A few days after Tracy's visit to the Pioneer Room, Don came running home, his face lighted up by excitement.

"Mother! Tracy!" he called as he burst into the kitchen. "Guess what? I've got the paper route!"

"Oh, goody!" Tracy cried.

"How nice," his mother said. "But how do you know?"

"I went over to the news agency again, and Mr. Nelson said I could try it for two weeks. I ought to be able to earn enough money for that party in two weeks, don't you think?"

His mother smiled and patted the top of his head. "Don't you worry about that, dear. We'll manage to make up the rest of the expense, you may be sure."

"Don't forget, you said I could help," Tracy reminded him.

"Sure, you can help if you want to—but do you think you'll be able to get up so early in the morning?"

Tracy thought it over, then reasoned: "It shouldn't be harder for me to get up, than it will be for you to get up."

"Oh, I don't know about that," Don insisted airily. "A job is a job."

Mr. Hill was pleased about the news, but he warned, "You'll have a pretty big route, young fellow. Maybe we could go over it for practice Saturday, just to get you acquainted."

"Thanks, Dad. That would be swell." Then Don added slowly, "On Monday when I start working, though, I'd like to be on my own."

Mr. Hill clapped him on the back. "You'll be on your own all right, son." He smiled at Mrs. Hill. "What's more, I have a hunch this boy of ours will always stand on his own two feet."

The news agency had arranged to drop off the papers for Don's route at a mailbox not far from home. When Saturday came, Mr. Hill took Don and Tracy over to that starting point. Then he drove to each house on Don's list, one at a time, so that they could get to know where they were going.

Early Monday when the alarm went off, it seemed as if it must surely be the middle of the night. Days were so short at this time of the year, full daylight had not yet come. Tracy dressed quickly but sleepily and, coming out into the hall, she met Don, looking every bit as sleepy as she was.

"Shh!" Tracy said, but Don was already saying, "Shh!" to her.

They tiptoed down the stairs, not wanting to wake their parents. They stopped only long enough to take some candy bars for themselves, and some carrots for Tizz.

They opened the kitchen door. There was an unexpected surprise. Fresh snow had fallen during the night, laying a thick white blanket over everything, lending an air of strangeness to the early morning.

Don and Tracy looked at each other. "Can you find your way?" Tracy asked.

"Sure," Don answered a little more loudly than he need have said it. "Come on."

As usual, Tizz sensed that something out of the ordinary was taking place. There she was, snorting in impatience as they came to get her.

"See how anxious she is to get started!" Tracy cried. "I think she knows that it's for her sake that you're taking the job—to earn the money for her party."

"*Her* party?" Don repeated.

"Yes. We're going to pay back the people who built her corral, so it *is* her party."

"Then she ought to pay for it," Don said in the quick way he had.

"She's working for her share of it, just as we are," Tracy pointed out, feeding Tizz her carrot while Don saddled her.

"Crunch, crunch," Tizz said, nodding her head as if the translation of those noises would be, "Most certainly!"

It was slippery going, but Tizz did not seem

to mind. Tracy rode her over to the starting point where the newspapers, dropped off before dawn by the man with the jeep, were waiting. Don climbed up to ride now and again but he did not mind plodding through the snow. Tizz carried the heavy canvas bag of rolled-up newspapers, and to Don, that was the main burden.

Delivering all the papers took a lot longer than they had imagined it would on Saturday when they had driven the rounds with their father. The going was slow on account of the snow, and Don had to be careful with the newspapers so that they would not get wet.

Quite often, when people saw the two approaching with Tizz, crunching their way through the snow and leaving deep tracks where there had been no tracks before, they came to the door or to the windows to wave a greeting. One kind woman gave each of them a cup of hot chocolate. Children ran out to say hello, and in several cases, they tagged along for a block or two.

The last paper was delivered and Don and

Tracy were heading for home when a familiar automobile came into sight. Knowing that car, they were not surprised to see that it was driven by their father, on his way to work.

"How did you do, kids?" he stopped to ask.

"Oh, fine," they answered as if they had been delivering papers every day of their lives.

"Your mother meant to give you breakfast. And I intended to drive you around this morning because of the snowstorm last night. But you were out so early and quietly that we never heard you."

Tracy and Don nudged each other. That was exactly what they had intended doing— getting out early, and on their own.

"Thanks just the same," Don said. "We got around all right, and we can have that breakfast when we get home."

"Tired?" their father asked as he started the car up again.

"Not a bit," they both answered at once.

As they went on towards home when their father was gone, Don said to Tracy, "It really was fun. There's only one thing I don't like about it. Getting up so early in the morning."

Tracy, yawning, admitted, "That's the only thing I don't like about it, too."

Tizz, trotting home to her feedbag and wanting to go faster, pulled at the reins, jerked her head, and whinnied.

"She's laughing," Tracy said.

Don agreed. "Sure," he teased, "she's giving us the horse laugh, because *she* doesn't mind getting up early."

It was true. Tizz did not mind at all. Not one bit.

OFF TO GRANDMA'S

Don and Tracy worked very hard for two weeks, getting up early to deliver newspapers every morning. Their mother was up early also, to be sure they had a warm breakfast before starting out. And their father put off buying the lumber for a work table he wanted to make, so that he could add that money to the party fund. Saying "thank you" for that corral of Tizz's had really become a family project!

Tizz, of course, worked hardest of all. She not only carried the newspapers, she also carried Tracy, and sometimes Don. It did not take her long to prove what a smart pony she was. Within a few days, she knew the route almost as well as Don, and would turn into a drive-way without a signal on the reins.

By the end of the week, something rather

special happened. When Don and Tracy were finishing up their paper route, a man with a camera got out of an automobile.

"Hi, kids!" he greeted them cheerily. "I'm from the *Morning Star*. One of our subscribers told us that you've been delivering papers with your pony."

"We couldn't do the job without Tizz," Don said quickly, giving Tizz full credit at once.

"Mind standing there for just a minute, so that I can get a picture?"

"For the *Star*?" Tracy asked, with wide eyes.

"Sure thing. I called your mother for permission first, and she said to go right ahead, if it is all right with you."

"Sure!" both Don and Tracy cried out in one voice.

Then Tracy giggled. "Maybe we'd better ask Tizz, though. She might not like it."

The photographer smiled over his camera. "I'm sure she won't have the slightest objection. Look at the way she's posing already."

And Tizz *was* posing! Or so it seemed. While

at rest, she had a habit of thrusting her right foreleg a bit ahead of the left one. Now there she was, obeying Tracy's hand on the reins, standing perfectly still, with one hoof daintily placed in front of the other.

Tracy stayed right where she was, up on Tizz's back. Don stood beside her, his hand resting on the canvas bag in which the papers were kept, and which was fastened to Tizz's saddle like a pack.

The photographer guessed as he snapped the picture, "This is going to be good!"

Briskly, he put the camera back in its case. Then he brought out a pad and pencil.

"Your name?" he asked Don first.

"Don Hill."

"And yours?" to Tracy.

"I'm Tracy Hill. And this is Tizz Hill. Don't forget to mention her."

"I won't." The photographer laughed. "You're quite a team."

He waved a hand in friendly fashion as he turned back to his car. "Well, have fun, kids."

"We will," Don called after him, "and thank you."

They could hardly wait until the next morning, to pick up their papers. For once, they did not mind getting up so early.

In spite of being eager, Don was careful about opening up one of the rolled newspapers in his pack. It would have to be delivered to someone on his route. He did not want to damage it the least bit.

There, on the back page, was the picture. A big one, too, taking up two columns. Tracy, wearing a wool scarf around her head to keep her ears from getting cold, was smiling proudly. Don, standing there in his leather jacket and cap with earmuffs, was more serious but just as proud. And Tizz! Well, there was Tizz with her right hoof poised daintily in front of the left one like the star of the show, her neck arched a little, displaying to the best advantage her beautiful white mane!

Delivering the newspapers that day was even more fun than ever. It seemed strange to Tracy and Don, to leave their own picture at every doorstep on their route.

By the time they got to school, all of their friends had seen the *Morning Star* and the picture. When Tracy came into her room, she noticed that Miss Brown had cut the picture out and placed it on the blackboard. There it was, for all to see, with the big print over the top:

PONY HELPS DELIVER PAPERS

She could read well enough to make out all the words under the picture, too:

Don and Tracy Hill have fun delivering the Morning Star with the help of their pet pony, Tizz. Neither snow nor cold have kept the children and their pony from doing their job.

Having the paper route was such an adventure that the children hated to give it up when Thanksgiving came, and it was time to drive down to the farm.

Mr. Nelson, the manager of the news agency, hated to have them give it up, too. "You've done a good job," he said when Don came in to see him at the end of the two weeks' trial period. "You can have that route all the time, if you want it."

"Thanks, but we're going to my grandparents' farm for Thanksgiving," Don reminded him.

"Yes, I remember you told me you were going. But I could have our man with the jeep take over the route until you come back, if you want to go on with it."

"Can I let you know after I come back?" Don asked after a second.

"Sure. Talk it over with your parents, then let me know."

Don supposed his mother and father would let him keep the job, if he wanted it. Yet he was not sure he wanted it, as a steady thing. Did he want to get up so early in the morning, all winter?

When he got home, he found that the rest of the family was waiting for him, ready to start out for the farm. The trailer was already attached to the car. Instead of talking about the paper route, Don helped Tracy lead Tizz out of the corral and into that trailer.

Tizz was just a tiny bit nervous about walking up the ramp, but as soon as she was inside, her nervousness seemed to drop from her. The pony looked around curiously, twitching her pretty tail excitedly, fully aware that something unusual was going on.

With Tizz settled, Tracy and Don got into the back seat of the car. Their father looked back to be sure they were all right. "All set?" he asked.

"All set," they answered in one voice.

There was a rumble of the engine, and the car started off. Looking back, Tracy could see Tizz swishing her tail happily.

They were off to Grandma's!

THANKSGIVING

It was quite late, at least for Tracy and Don, when the car and trailer pulled into the driveway that led to the house set back of the road. Even in the dark, the children could recognize that familiar house.

"Hurray, we're there!" Don cried.

"I wonder if Grandma is waiting up?" Tracy asked.

She needn't have wondered. Of course her grandmother was waiting up! So was her grandfather. There they were, on the porch, waving eagerly. They had stepped out of the well-lighted house as soon as the car had turned in.

It was easy to tell, from their outlines, which figure was that of their grandmother, and which, their grandfather. One was tiny, the other tall. Both had a young-looking straightness.

Tracy and Don tumbled out of the automobile as soon as it came to a stop. In a moment they were racing up the steps of the farmhouse, shouting, "Hello, Grandma! Hello, Grandpa!"

Grandma could hug awfully strong, for a little woman. Grandpa swung Tracy up in the air like a bell, but when he turned to Don, he decided, "Nope, getting too big for that. Guess you and I will just have to shake hands from now on!"

"Come in, come in," Grandma was saying, and, in the same sentence, "My but it's good to see you again."

"We brought Tizz along," Tracy reminded her, hesitating about going into the house.

"Yes, I know." Grandma nodded. "We knew you couldn't go off and leave her alone."

"We've got a place all ready for her in the barn," Grandpa chimed in. "Andy's all set to take care of her."

There, right on cue, was Andy, the hired man, coming around the corner of the house from the barn. "Howdy, folks!" he called.

"Hello, Andy," everyone said, and Mrs. Hill added in her friendly way, "It's good to see you again."

"I'm glad to see you, too, Andy" Tracy spoke up, "but if you don't mind, I'd like to take care of Tizz myself tonight. She might be a little nervous in a strange place."

Mrs. Hill laughed. "You might as well let her bed down that pony herself. Otherwise, she'll be worrying half the night."

"Why don't both of you children go along with Andy, and then come into the house?" Grandma suggested. "I just happen to have some cookies and fresh milk on hand."

Tracy and Don helped Andy lead Tizz from the trailer to a stall in the barn. The pony seemed eager to leave the trailer, but when she smelled the horses in the barn, she snorted in quite an unladylike manner. After all, she was quite young, and was used to being in her quarters alone. She was not sure she liked strangers.

Tracy knew just how to handle her. She

talked to Tizz gently, and patted her neck. Don helped, too. He patted her withers, and they coaxed her into the stall without any trouble. Once in it, Tizz relaxed and made herself at home.

Tracy relaxed then, too. After her snack of fresh milk and homemade cookies, she went upstairs to the room where she always slept when she visited the farm. It was a small room, just the right size for a small girl. There was nothing in it but a narrow bed, a dresser with a marble top, a braided rag rug, and a small old-fashioned rocker that she dearly loved.

Tonight, the room seemed cold, because the farmhouse did not have the kind of heating Tracy was used to. Once in her warm pajamas and in the thick downy featherbed, though, she grew warm quickly. In fact, she was sound asleep even before her mother could tiptoe out of the room.

The minute she woke up the next morning, Tracy knew it was Thanksgiving Day. Her room was directly over the kitchen, and all the

delicious odors that belonged to this special day drifted up through the floor. Just lying there and sniffing, Tracy could guess what they were going to have for dinner. The turkey was already in the oven. Chestnut dressing? Yes, hurray! Those spices meant pumpkin pies, and that rich fragrance, mince.

Although Tracy hurried down to the kitchen, Don was already out of the house. Grandma, working at the big cookstove, took time out to whip up a batch of pancakes, which she served swimming in a wonderful hot sauce made up of melted butter, maple syrup, honey and cinnamon.

"You'll have to eat a dozen, to beat Don," Grandma said.

Tracy shook her head. "Not on Thanksgiving, Grandma! I want to save room for that turkey."

All the same, she did quite well by the pancakes. Then she hurried out-of-doors to see Tizz and to find Don and the menfolk. They were all together, in the barn. Don had already given Tizz her breakfast, and now he, his father, his grandfather and the hired man were all examining a young steer that was going to be entered in a livestock show.

Tracy thought the animal was fine looking, but personally she preferred a mother cat playing with her kittens. They were all striped in a golden yellow, and she thought they looked as if they wearing matching mother-and-daughter dresses.

The talk about the livestock show gave Tracy an idea. "We ought to enter Tizz in a pony show."

Grandpa turned his smile in her direction. "Tizz is a pretty pony, Tracy, but to tell the truth, all ponies look pretty to me. Wait till you see all of them at the pony farm."

"The pony farm!" Don cried. "Are we going there?"

"Yes, your grandmother and I thought we'd go over there tomorrow."

Tracy jumped for joy. "Oh, I can't wait."

"I'm afraid you'll have to," Grandfather

smiled. He turned to the rest of the party. "Well, how about a walk, to work up a big appetite for that turkey dinner?"

"I'll ride Tizz," Tracy decided. "She needs the exercise."

They all set out across the hard fields, Tracy on the pony, the others on foot. The brown landscape was marked here and there by patches of snow. It was crisply cold but not bitter, and Tracy did not mind at all. Only her fingers and toes felt a little nippy, when it was time to go back.

They could hear the dinner bell ringing as they neared the farmhouse, so they hurried in and washed up quickly. Then everyone marched into the dining room. Not Tracy and Don, of course. They ran. When they got there, however, they politely waited until the grown-ups were seated, then took their places themselves.

Tracy's blue eyes grew wide as they looked over the beautiful table, dressed up with a fruit centerpiece, and Grandma's best china and silver and linen. At one end, where Grandpa

sat, there was just about the most enormous turkey she had ever seen. It was golden-brown all over, and the golden juice was seeping out of it into the hollow part of the big platter. Also on the table were bowls of vegetables and relishes, and Grandma's fluffy yeast rolls.

Then Tracy lowered her eyes, as the others were doing. Grandpa's head was bowed, and

in a deep, solemn voice, he said: "Lord, we thank Thee for Thy bounty, and ask Thy blessing on this table."

Tracy raised her eyes again. They met Don's. She saw that his were serious, as hers were. She knew that Don, too, was realizing that there was a great deal more to Thanksgiving than good things to eat.

PONY FARM

After dinner, Tracy felt as if she could hardly move away from the table. Don expressed her thoughts exactly when he said, "Wow! That was the best Thanksgiving dinner I ever ate!"

His father added, "I've had a lot more Thanksgiving dinners than you've had, son, and I can second the motion."

Grandma flushed with pleasure, but she said modestly, "Oh, come now, you say that every year!"

"Every year it seems a little bit better than the year before," Mrs. Hill insisted. "I hope some day I'll be as good a cook, Mother, but that's a lot to hope for."

"Not at all," Grandma insisted. "You're well on your way already."

Tracy said loyally. "I think Mother is the

best cook in the whole world — next to you, Grandma."

Grandpa kissed Tracy on the top of her head. "Here's a girl who's going to grow up to be a real diplomat."

Tracy thought it over. Whatever a diplomat was, it sounded important. "If I'm a diplomat, can I still ride Tizz?"

"If Tizz will let you, by that time," Grandma smiled.

"Oh, Tizz will always let me. She likes to have me ride her."

Thinking of Tizz, Tracy decided to go out to the barn and see her pony. "Don't you think she ought to have something special, for her Thanksgiving dinner?" she wanted to know.

"Yes, and I've got just the thing," Grandpa said in his hearty voice. "You come along with me, Tracy, and help pick it out."

Tracy skipped along with her grandfather. They went back of the house, and down a few steps into what was called a root cellar. Here, some of the vegetables grown on the farm

during the summer were stored for family use.

"Look at those carrots," Grandpa said. "Did you ever see prettier ones?"

"No," Tracy agreed, "and I'm sure Tizz never did, either. How many may she have, Grandpa?"

"How many do you think she could eat, without being greedy?"

"Tizz *can* be greedy," Tracy confessed. "Maybe I'd better give her just these two big ones now, and some more tomorrow."

Grandpa nodded. "That seems like a good idea."

Tracy told Tizz all about the wonderful

Thanksgiving dinner she had enjoyed, while the pony munched carrots. Tizz seemed to be listening to every word that was said. She shook her head now and again, but from the way she enjoyed those carrots, Tracy could tell that she would not have traded Thanksgiving dinners for anything in the world.

The next day, the whole family went over to the pony farm. Mr. and Mrs. Hill and Grandma and Grandpa rode in the car. Tracy and Don took turns riding Tizz. No one would have thought of leaving Tizz at home, of course. She had come from the pony farm, and Tracy especially wanted her to have a chance to visit it.

She talked to Tizz about it, along the way. "Grandma said she didn't think you'd remember, but I'm sure that you will. I only hope," she added with a worried note in her voice, "that you won't like it so much that you'll want to stay there with all of your friends and relations."

The pony farm was a delightful place, spread out along gently rolling hills, with a brook that

would wind through when it was not frozen over. There were corrals for the ponies, where they were turned out to exercise each day.

About forty ponies were in the corrals when the company arrived. Tracy and Don had never seen so many all at one time. Some were cream-colored like Tizz.

"All those cream-colored ones look like Tizz," Mrs. Hill said as the family watched the ponies.

"Oh, no, Mother, they don't!" Tracy said in a hurt voice. Why, she could tell Tizz anywhere!

The owner of the farm, who was a friend of Tracy's grandparents, came out to visit for a while. He was very pleased with Tizz's appearance. "She's a fine pony, and you've taken very good care of her," he praised. He looked from

Don to Tracy. "Which one of you is in charge?" he asked with a smile.

"We both are," Tracy answered.

"Sometimes Tracy has more time to exercise her," Don added, "but I always help with the currying and feeding."

The pony farm owner nodded. "That sounds like a good arrangement."

He put an arm on Tracy's shoulder and directed her attention towards a pretty pony, bigger than Tizz, at the far end of the corral.

"See that one over there? Well she's your pony's mother."

Tracy's voice came out in a burst of surprise. "She is!"

Her hand went to Tizz's mane. "Look, Tizz, that's your mother over there! Don't you want to go in and visit her?"

The pony farm owner shook his head. "They wouldn't know each other. I'll tell you what I'd like to do, though. When Tizz is ready to be bred, I'd like to have her back here. I've got a stallion who would make a fine sire."

"I'll bet pony colts are awfully cute," Mrs. Hill exclaimed.

"Yes, they certainly are. We don't have any real young ones now because this is not the season, but you've never seen anything sweeter than a bunch of pony colts frisking about together."

Tracy was silent for a moment, carried away by the wonderful thought that someday, Tizz might be a mother.

"Why, Tizz," she said at last, "you'd make a perfectly wonderful mother!"

"I don't know about that," Mr. Hill said.

"Not the way she's been acting, always getting into mischief."

"But that was before she had her corral. She'll never get into mischief again. Will you, Tizz?"

Tizz pawed the hard ground with a dainty hoof, and neighed.

"You've hurt her feelings, Daddy," Tracy said, patting her pony's neck lovingly.

Mr. Hill looked at his mother with a smile. "You see? That's the way it is, all the time."

Grandma smiled, and shrugged calmly. "All the same," she spoke up, "getting that pony was the best thing in the world for those children."

"You said it, Grandma!" Don burst out.

Tracy murmured a heartfelt and more polite, "That's true." She curled her fingers into Tizz's mane, protectively, as if she never intended to let her go. She was delighted that Tizz belonged in the Hill family and was not milling about in the corral with all those other ponies. They were pretty, yes, but Tracy was convinced that Tizz was the most beautiful of them all.

PILGRIMS THREE

Riding back to their grandparents' farm, Tracy was thinking about how happy she was to have such a beautiful pony as Tizz, but Don's thoughts were somewhere else.

Tracy knew his thoughts were really quite far away when he spoke up suddenly: "They really had it pretty hard."

It was with a little wrench that Tracy brought her mind around to what Don had said. "Who had it pretty hard?"

"Why, the Pilgrims, of course. All the pioneers, for that matter."

"When we went to the Pioneer Room, we pretended we were living in pioneer times," Tracy remembered. "We did just what they used to do. It was fun."

"Bet it wouldn't be fun if you had to do it

every day," Don argued. "On the other hand," he went on, his mind racing ahead with the different ideas that were coming to him, "I'd kind of like to be able to shoot a turkey whenever I wanted one."

"What if there weren't any turkeys," Tracy wondered out loud.

"Of course there were turkeys. Millions of 'em, I betcha!"

Dreamily, talking in time to the rhythm of Tizz's easy gait, Tracy said: "Wouldn't it be fun to play we were Pilgrims, the way we played we were pioneers?"

Don caught up the idea at once. "Sure!" he agreed. "Why don't we?" Again, his mind raced ahead. "Let's put on a play about it, the way we do on Cub Scout Pack Night. We could ask Grandma and Grandpa, and Mother and Dad."

"And Andy," Tracy added loyally. She liked the hired man, who did many favors for her.

"Where will we have it?"

Tracy thought it over. "In the barn?"

"Why the barn?"

"Because I don't think Grandma would want Tizz to come into the house."

"What has Tizz got to do with it?"

Tracy's voice tingled. "Why, we couldn't have a play without having Tizz in it! She'd be awfully hurt. Wouldn't you, Tizz?"

Tizz nodded.

"Look," Tracy pointed out, "she's saying yes."

"Of course she's saying yes," Don said. "You're pulling her reins too tight!"

"Even so," Tracy insisted, "she'd be hurt."

"Okay, okay," Don said in a might-as-well-make-the-best-of-it kind of voice. "Tizz can be in it, too. Only trouble is—if we're going to drive back home real early tomorrow morning, we'd better put it on this afternoon."

"We'll have to rehearse first."

Don agreed, and they got to work as soon as they returned to the farm. First they "warned" the family that there would be a play later in the afternoon.

In the barn, there was a big space that would do nicely as a theatre. The "audience" could sit comfortably on big bales of hay, and there was enough room for the actors.

Don was still puzzled about Tizz's part in the play. "I don't remember that any ponies came along on the Mayflower, from what I've read or heard," he said, wrinkling his forehead as he usually did when he was deep in thought.

Then he rapped his head with his forefinger and exclaimed: "I've got it! Tizz can *be* the Mayflower!"

"The boat?"

"Sure! She's good and solid, just like the Mayflower was."

Tracy thought over the idea and decided she liked it. They made two big "sails" for Tizz out of old newspapers, and fastened them on each side of her collar. After practicing in the barn several times, they called the family together.

When everybody, including Andy the hired man, was ready, the play began. Don stepped out into the big space he considered the stage, and said very solemnly:

"Good afternoon, ladies and gentlemen. You are about to witness the landing of the Pilgrims at Plymouh Rock. As they say on television— You Are There!"

He ran off to the doorway, where Tracy and Tizz were waiting. After he had leaped on Tizz's back, behind Tracy, she slowly guided the pony through the door and into the circle of space before the audience.

"Here comes the Mayflower!" Don called from Tizz's back, in a special deep kind of voice which Tracy thought sounded just like the man on television.

Tizz approached slowly, her sails and "passengers" swaying from side to side.

"That boat seems to be rocking pretty badly." Grandpa observed with a smile.

"Certainly," Grandmother nodded. "The seas were rough that day."

When Tizz was right in front of the audience, Tracy brought her to a halt. She and Don alighted and pretended to anchor the "boat." Tizz seemed surprised at the unusual procedure, but stood her ground, like the very good pony she was learning to be.

An unrehearsed scene was enacted by the two big farm horses who were in their stalls. Seeing the strange pony entering the barn with even stranger looking "sails" attached to her halter, they began to snort and whinny. Because they were so big, their nervous, restless pawing made quite an offstage noise.

Other farm animals joined in the racket, so that for a few minutes there was quite a bit of confusion.

"The Indians are about to attack," Grandpa said from the sidelines.

Don picked up the cue at once. "Priscilla," he said seriously, "methinks there might be redskins about. Do you know how to use a shooting iron?"

"I sure do," Tracy replied, then quickly corrected herself to say primly instead, "Yes, John, I do have an understanding of it."

She accepted the make-believe rifle and then she and Don went on with their story of the landing of the Pilgrims as soon as the racket died down. Together they chose a place to live, cleared a place in the wilderness, built a cabin with their own hands—all in gestures which cleverly put across their meaning, as they had no props. Then they tilled the soil and planted corn. Finally, there was the harvest and the feast day when they gave thanks.

As Tracy was setting the Thanksgiving table, Don remembered that he had forgotten to shoot the turkey. "Excuse me, Priscilla," he said quickly with great stage presence, "I think I'll go out and shoot a turkey."

He hurried off a few paces, said "Bang-bang" into the loft of the barn, and returned carrying a fine, if imaginary, bird.

Tracy showed equal presence of mind. "Well, John," she said calmly when Don handed her the pretend-turkey, "dinner may be a little late, but I'm sure it will be well worth waiting for."

Don brought the playlet to a close by saying

grace at the make-believe table when "dinner" was ready. He said almost the same words Grandpa had said yesterday, and as he spoke, his voice sounded so much like his grandfather's that Grandma murmured, "How sweet!"

Every one thought the play was awfully good. Grandma said, "You'd better come into the house and have some cookies. I understand actors get very hungry after a play."

"Don't you think Tizz should have a carrot?" Tracy asked. "Being the Mayflower was hard work."

"Yes, certainly she must have a carrot," Grandma readily agreed.

"To tell the truth," Don said as he thought it over, "being a Pilgrim was hard work, too. I think I'd rather be living right now."

"So would I," Tracy said. Being a Pilgrim had been fun for a while, just as playing pio - neer had been fun for a while. But for everyday life, she'd rather be Tracy Hill, a girl with a pony named Tizz.

THE SQUARE DANCE

Early the next morning, the Hills started for home. Tracy and Don hated to leave their grandparents, but they promised to come up for a visit soon.

"At least your Grandmother will come," Grandpa added. "It's pretty hard for me to get away, you know. But you'll be down for another visit soon, maybe during spring vacation, or certainly in the summertime."

"Spring is a long way off," Tracy said mournfully.

"Oh, fiddlesticks!" Grandma laughed. "Spring will be here in no time at all." It was easy to see, though, that she was pleased at the thought of being missed.

Tizz was led into the trailer after the car was packed and everyone was ready to go. This time she went up the ramp without hesitating at all, and again she looked about curiously, eager for her adventure to begin.

The morning was cold and gray. "This is just about the time I'd be delivering papers, back home," Don said as they were driving along the highway.

"Glad the job is over, son?"

"N-n-no, not exactly," Don answered slowly. Then he added, "Mr. Nelson said I could have the route all the time, if I wanted it."

"Good for you!" his mother praised from the front seat. "That proves you did a good job."

"Tracy, too," Don put in loyally.

"Yes, Tracy too, of course," Mrs. Hill seconded quickly.

"Do you want it Don?" Mr. Hill asked. "You kids have earned all I'm going to let you pitch in as your share of that party we'll have, you know."

"Yes, but I've been thinking—in the spring, we're going to go on some overnights with our Cub Scout Troop. We'll need sleeping bags and all kinds of equipment. I could earn the money for that equipment, if I kept the paper route."

"You hate to get up so early in the morning," Tracy reminded him.

"So what?" Don retorted. Then he smiled as he admitted, "You know that play we put on yesterday, about the Pilgrims? It made me feel kind of silly, being such a sissy about getting up so early to do something easy like delivering newspapers."

Tracy nodded in brisk agreement. "That's the way I felt after we went to the Pioneer Room. They had it so much harder than we do."

"Sure. After thinking about what they had to go through, getting up real early doesn't seem like anything at all."

"Can I keep on helping you, Don?" Tracy asked eagerly.

Their father spoke up thoughtfully. "No, Tracy, you'd better not. It was all right for you to help Don for awhile, to earn the money for the party you both wanted. That was a joint project. But it was Don who got the paper route, and he's the one who should have the right to go on with it if he chooses to do so."

"Then it's all right if I tell Mr. Nelson tomorrow that I'd like to keep the job?" Don asked.

"It certainly is all right, son. And I'm proud of you for wanting to keep it."

"I'm proud of Tizz," Tracy said. "She's going to keep her job, too."

Mr. Hill chuckled. "By golly, she will, won't she? She's got to, if Don is to get around!"

"If you let me take Tizz on the paper route every morning, you can have her for yourself every afternoon," Don bargained.

Tracy thought it over. "All right. That's fair. But you've got to take good care of her!"

Mrs. Hill laughed. "Don't worry, Tracy. Don loves that pony as much as you do. Now let's talk about that party. When shall we have it, and what kind of a party shall it be?"

They talked it over excitedly while the automobile clicked off the miles. By the time the

Hills got back home, everything was settled. It would be a square dance, with the children invited as well as their parents. The furniture would be pushed aside to make room for dancing. A supper would be served.

The very next day, Tracy and Don helped get out the invitations. They used colored paper and carefully helped print:

There's going to be a Square Dance.
Where? At the Hills.
When? Friday.
Time? 5:30.
    You All Come!

When Tracy hurried home from school on the day of the party, the kitchen was as full of lovely fragrances as Grandma's kitchen on the farm. A great big kettle of spaghetti sauce was cooking on the range, and the refrigerator was full of trays of a jellied fruit salad. There would also be spaghetti for the sauce when the time came, and hot rolls made from Grandma's recipe, and a big bowl of crunchy relishes, and dozens and dozens of those great big melty chocolate-chip cookies which Tracy especially loved.

She and Don pitched in to help set up the tables and get everything ready. By then, their father came home, and it was time to wash up and change.

It was only after she had dressed in her white blouse and full ruffled skirt that Tracy realized something terrible had happened. She had forgotten all about Tizz! For the first time.

"Don't worry about it," Don assured her. "I fed her when I came home."

"Yes, but she'll be lonesome."

"I don't think she'll mind, for once," her mother comforted. Then, as the doorbell rang: "Well, here are the first guests!"

For a while, the family was so busy helping to serve everyone that Tracy couldn't think about Tizz. The supper was awfully good, and many went back for second, and even third, helpings. Earlier in the day Tracy had thought no one would ever be able to eat up that mountain of food, but by the time everyone had had enough, there was very little left. In fact, after she and Don made the last trip to the kitchen, there was nothing at all left!

The music began. Mrs. Hill played the piano, and Sue's father played a violin. Mr. Hill was the square-dance caller.

Suddenly, Tracy could not bear the thought of having fun without Tizz. Quietly, she slipped out of the house the kitchen way, stopping to pick up a bunch of carrots. At the corral she found Tizz at the gate, curiously watching the house and listening to the music.

Tracy knew just what Tizz wanted, she was sure. She put on the pony's halter rope. In it, she tucked the bunch of carrots, saying, "This is your corsage for the party." Then she led her out of the corral, into the garage, and through the garage door that led into the kitchen.

No one saw Tracy come in until she had led the pony into the hall separating the dining room from the living room. Then, everyone seemed to see her at once, and a loud cry went up: "Tizz!"

"Good heavens, what next?" Mr. Hill cried. "Tracy, take that pony out of the house!"

"But this is her party!" Tracy protested.

"Of course it's her party," the neighbors agreed.

Tracy looked towards her mother. "Couldn't she stay just a little while?" she begged.

Her mother and father exchanged a glance, and Mrs. Hill suggested, "As long as she's in, suppose we let her stay a few minutes?"

Mr. Hill gave in. "All right."

For those few minutes, Tizz was the life of the party. She stood there in the hall, not being in anybody's way, just watching the dancing and listening to the music. She seemed to be having the time of her life.

Tracy looked away for a few minutes, and when she looked back, she found that Tizz was eating the bunch of carrots. "Oh, Tizz!" she

cried, "you're eating your corsage! Now you have nothing special for the party."

Tracy ran up to her room quickly and brought down her best blue satin hair ribbon. This she fastened on top of Tizz's beautiful white mane. Tizz swished her head, showing off the hair ribbon, delighted that she, too, was dressed for a party.

When the time was up, Tizz bowed out of the hall very politely as Tracy led her back through the kitchen door and the garage, into the corral. As soon as the halter rope was removed, Tizz scampered away in high spirits, the satin ribbon which Tracy had forgotten to take off, bouncing merrily in the wind.

Back in the house, Tracy joined in the dancing and the fun. She was happy now, because she knew Tizz was happy.

"It's a swell party!" Don whispered when he had a chance.

"Yes, 'tis," Tracy answered. Then, remembering what Miss Brown had said in school some weeks before, she added, "That's what it *is* for!"

"What what is for?" Don asked with a puzzled look.

"T. It's for Tizz."

"Who said it wasn't?" Don retorted.

He grabbed her around the waist, shouted, "And away we go!" and whirled her around in the square dance number. Her pony tail bobbed up and down, just like Tizz's.